Barnaby Barchart's Beach Adventure

A VizKidz Story

by Liv Buli   Illustrated by Mark Carey

Meet Barnaby Barchart.

He's always collecting and comparing the bits and pieces he comes across.

Today Barnaby is at the beach with his friends.

"Let's hunt for treasure," Barnaby says.

"And then we'll use my backpack to count who collected the most!"

The rest of the Vizkidz set off
to search for their favorite treasures.

"Look what I found! Four shovels no less."

Bertie Boxplot thinks crabs make a bit of a mess.

OUCH!

"Yes, they do! I found 1, 2, 3, 4, 5, 6, 7 seashells," Barnaby brags. He is certain that he can't be beat!

"But how will we know who has collected the most?" asks Bertie.

Barnaby has a plan for this gathered treasure.

"We'll put it in my backpack and that will help us measure!"

It's Confusion Curmudgeon with his arms full of coins.
"Can I play, too?"

"Wow!" says Barnaby.
"You sure did collect a lot of treasure."

"I guess I didn't win after all."

"Aha!" Bertie has an idea.
"How about we take one of those
coins and buy some ice cream?"

Now Barnaby and Curmudgeon both have seven!

"Hooray!" shout the Vizkidz. "It's a perfect day for ice cream and treasure hunts at the beach!"

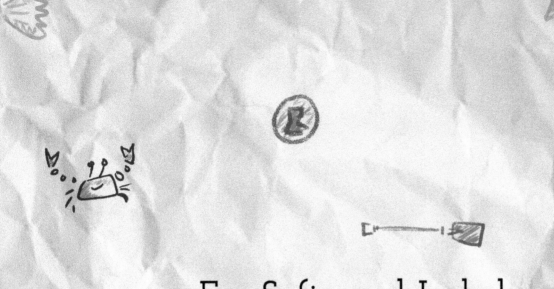

For Sofie and Isabel

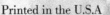

Printed in the U.S.A

CPSIA information can be obtained
at www.ICGtesting.com
Printed in the USA
LVHW072027070519
617021LV00005B/10/P